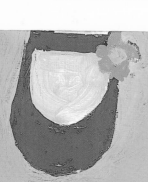

For Christiné—
special friends are always treasured.

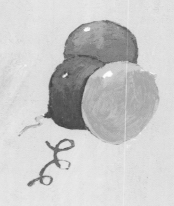

Orchard Books, A Grolier Company
95 Madison Avenue, New York, NY 10016

Manufactured in Singapore
The text of this book is set in 60 point Blockhead Unplugged.
The illustrations are gouache.
3 5 7 9 10 8 6 4 2

Library of Congress cataloging-in-publication data is available upon request.

ISBN 0-531-30268-7   LC 99-48058

New Shoes, Red Shoes

Susan Rollings

ORCHARD BOOKS   NEW YORK

Two shoes,
small shoes.

Off to get some
new shoes.

Low shoes, high shoes.

Sitting on the bus shoes.

Flat shoes,
summer shoes.

Friends with
very pointy shoes.

Warm shoes,
soft shoes.

Tiny little baby shoes.

Tired shoes,
    dirty shoes.

Rows and rows
and rows of shoes.

Blue shoes,
pink shoes.

Red and shiny
new shoes.

Best shoes,
    special shoes.

Home with
very precious shoes.

New shoes,
party shoes.

Time to put them on shoes.

Happy shoes,
dancing shoes.

Skipping to the party shoes.

Ribbon shoes,
sparkly shoes.

Big and
noisy racing shoes.

Magic shoes,
disco shoes.

Mustn't step on
these new shoes.

Lots and lots
and lots of shoes.

But best of all
are MY shoes!